Stories for the 12 Days of Christmas

Stories for the 12 Days of Christmas

Linda Mansfield

A Restart Communications, LLC publication

First published in the United States by Linda Mansfield.

STORIES FOR THE 12 DAYS OF CHRISTMAS

ISBN: 978-0-9962433-2-2 (EPUB)

ISBN: 978-0-9962433-3-9 (MOBI)

ISBN: 978-0-9962433-1-5 (paperback)

ISBN: 978-0-9962433-0-8 (hardcover)

Cover art © Konstiantyn/Dollar Photo Club.

10 9 8 7 6 5 4 3 2 1

For you.

Take a break!

Contents

Introduction

Indianapolis, Indiana

Let's face it. Despite the song that claims it's the most wonderful time of the year, the Christmas season is full of stress.

I want to give you a break. You're holding a baker's dozen of short stories with a Christmas theme, featuring people from assorted walks of life.

Some of the stories may make you smile. Others are more serious.

Although the stories are fiction, I tried to make them as realistic as possible. No flying reindeer, dancing snowmen, Grinches (at least not the green ones), or elves are involved.

There is a great deal of love throughout this little book, but these tales are not romances. There are plenty of Christmas books that cover that. This one is different.

No story is more than 2,000 words, because I know you're busy. The 11th and 12th stories should be read together, but the order of the others doesn't matter. I threw in a 13th one because I like to give people more than they expect, at Christmas and otherwise.

I like to imagine that you're reading this book in a recliner in front of a crackling fire, with a plate of cookies and a mug of hot cocoa or mulled wine on the end table beside you. But that would probably be a stretch, if not a real Christmas miracle.

There are different opinions about when the 12 Days of Christmas begin. Please don't stress about it. Do whatever works best for you. If you'd like, you can read one story daily during the 12 days leading up to Christmas, although there are no partridges in this book either. You can read one story daily on the 12 days after Christmas. You can start on Christmas Eve. You can also read one story every now and then throughout the year when you get around to dusting the bookshelves. Or you can read the whole book at once on some electronic gizmo while you're waiting for a delayed flight.

I do hope you enjoy these stories, though. It's my Christmas wish that they'll make your holidays a little brighter, a little less stressful, and they'll remind you of the real reason for the season.

Merry Christmas!

Linda Mansfield

1

It's Better to Give Than to Receive

With her right foot on the brake, Kathy Simpson grabbed the passenger-side headrest with her right hand, quickly twisted her body, and looked out of the dirty rear window of her battered, dull-green compact car. No one else was in the alley except for a gray cat prowling on top of a dumpster. Kathy quickly slipped her right hand back onto the automatic gear shifter, threw the car into reverse, looked out the rear window again, took her foot off the brake, slowly moved it onto the accelerator, and carefully backed out of her parking space. The car rumbled and belched like a stock car as she paused and pulled it into drive. Its muffler was just one of many of its components that needed attention, but at least today the old bag of bolts started.

Kathy was already working two jobs to make ends meet. She didn't have money for a new muffler or time for any trouble.

But she had to make time for this.

Yesterday she'd received a call from Martha Bruce, whom she'd known since both attended Mainsville Elementary. These days

Martha was the school's fourth-grade teacher, and she wanted Kathy to stop by for a "chat" about Kathy's only child, Luke, who was 9.

The school was about three miles from Kathy's apartment above one of only two restaurants in town, The Brown Jug, where she was a waitress.

She'd also been a cashier at Mainsville's sole dollar store since it opened five years ago to serve the rural Indiana town. The locals jokingly referred to the small store as "The Mainsville Mall." The nearest real mall was in Grantville, a 75-minute drive north.

Mainsville was so small it didn't even appeal to Walmart. The only "bright lights" of this town were the lights that blinked on the gas station's soda machine when it ran out of cans.

Being a single mother in a one-horse town like Mainsville wasn't the life Kathy had anticipated, but the gods of destiny had a different plan. It had taken her too long to realize that despite his many charms, not the least of which was a killer smile, Luke's father was a loser.

Luke's father's whereabouts had been unknown for about eight months now. The whereabouts of the alimony checks he was supposed to send monthly had also been unknown going on a year and a half.

Luke had his father's sapphire-blue eyes, his dazing smile, and an upbeat demeanor. Kathy knew that just like his dad, he wouldn't lack for female companions. But Kathy was determined that Luke would have a solid upbringing. Unlike his dad, he'd grow up to be a good person, even if it killed her.

That's if she didn't kill him first for getting into trouble at school.

Martha was erasing the blackboard when Kathy walked into the classroom. Although Martha had no children of her own, she was patient and well suited to the demands of teaching children.

"How are you, Kathy?" Martha asked as she put the eraser on the ledge at the bottom of the blackboard. She settled her large frame into the chair at her desk and motioned for Kathy to take the chair next to it.

"Oh, you know, just another day in paradise," Kathy said, smoothing a section of her shoulder-length brown hair behind her left ear as she sat down. Although she'd known Martha almost all her life, she wasn't sure what to do with her hands, so she just folded them on her lap. Her brown vinyl hobo bag dropped to the floor beside the chair.

"Did he get into a fight with one of the Briggs boys again?"

"No; he's not in trouble, but there's something going on that I think you should know about," Martha said.

"He's not eating lunch," she announced. "He's saving his lunch money for a new Colts football jacket instead."

Kathy took a few beats to comprehend this revelation. With the school's federal and state budget allocations, a school lunch cost $2.40. It would take quite awhile to save up enough money for a $100 jacket licensed by the NFL.

"I should explain that better," Martha continued. "He is eating some lunch, because his friends are giving him the parts of their lunches they don't like.

"He's probably eating more healthy than they are," she added with a smile.

"What should I do about it?" Kathy asked.

"For now, I'd say nothing," Martha advised. "Let's see how long it lasts. He definitely wants that jacket. But even at 9 he knows it's a luxury. You have a perceptive boy in Luke, that's for sure."

"I got him a new jacket before school started last year, and I bought it in a larger size than he needed so it would last a couple of years," Kathy thought aloud, wrapping her hands into and out of a knot.

"Kids change their minds easily and go on to something else,"

Martha replied kindly. "I know times are tough. I just wanted you to know what was going on."

"Thank you," Kathy said earnestly.

With that she glanced down at the watch she'd worn since junior high, and realized she only had 15 minutes to make it to The Brown Jug to start her shift on time. She said a quick goodbye and was on her way, but her mind was busy contemplating her meager monthly budget and the unending bills.

She clocked in 5 minutes late, and her shoulders were lower than usual as she put on her tan apron, grabbed her notepad and pen, and headed to her first table. She already had a few Christmas gifts for Luke, but she would return them and concentrate on buying him that jacket. She was determined that Luke would have a great Christmas, with or without his dad.

Kathy knew her mother would help. She cared for Luke each day after school and made him supper more often than not, since Kathy was usually at the restaurant in the evenings.

A few days passed before she could mention it to her mother, though. That same night when Luke came home from her mother's house a few doors down the street he was holding an ice pack over his left eye. When Kathy asked him how he got the shiner, at first he said he fell. Later, when she checked on him at bedtime, he admitted he was on the losing end of an argument with Barry Briggs.

Barry was 11, and this wasn't the first time the two had scuffled.

Although the area around his eye was already black and blue, with a little tinge of yellow, this time his eye wasn't swollen shut.

"What happened?" Kathy asked him gently, wiping the long, blond hair on Luke's forehead out of the inflamed area.

"He said I was a loser, and I have elephant ears," Luke said, sniffling. "I told him to take it back. He wouldn't, and he said some other stuff too. He needs to learn a lesson," Luke added with all the defiance a 9-year-old boy could muster, tilting his chin up for emphasis.

Kathy suspected "the other stuff" Barry had said was worse, but she needed to make a point.

"Fighting doesn't solve problems, does it?" she asked gently. "I think Barry is a troubled young man. He doesn't have nearly as many friends as you have, does he?" she pointed out. "We need to try to love our enemies, and be kind to them, as hard as that can be," she added. "Now try to get some sleep, because it will be morning before you know it!"

After a hug and a quick kiss, she closed his bedroom door, walked down the hall, sat down in front of an old laptop, and went shopping.

The Colts jacket cost $89.95 on line, with an extra $4.99 for shipping. It wouldn't be easy, but she'd make it happen. One of the other cashiers at the dollar store was due to go on maternity leave, so she'd be able to get some more hours there. Hopefully her car's muffler would last at least until the spring. Kathy wasn't sure when she'd sleep, and she hated to miss any more time with Luke than she normally did, but he was going to have that jacket.

Kathy never let on that she knew about Luke's lunch money savings plan, but when Martha stopped into The Brown Jug for a quick dinner two weeks before Christmas, she said it was still in effect.

"He's eating a lot of beans, stewed tomatoes, and coleslaw," Martha disclosed with a smile.

Luke finally had enough of that diet a week later, and one night he tried a more direct approach.

"Mom, do you know what I want from Santa this year?" he asked when she checked on him after her mother had already put him to bed. Kathy was bone tired from a busy shift at The Brown Jug after a full day at the dollar store.

"I thought you didn't believe in Santa anymore?" Kathy responded cagily, tucking his blue comforter firmly around his body.

"Well, just in case, I'd like a Colts jacket," he announced. "A black one, with a hood, and 'Colts' on the back."

Kathy had ordered the jacket more than a week ago, but she was good at being coy. The electric bill would be late this month and next, and she'd have to be even more careful than usual when grocery shopping, but the jacket was on its way to her P.O. box.

"Well, it's better to give than to receive," she replied. It was all she could think of to say.

Luke's brilliant blue eyes dove to the bed's footboard as he avoided his mother's gaze.

"That's what I want, anyway," he said, as his voice trailed off.

The long hours at both the store and the restaurant took their toll. Kathy tried to stay on an even keel, but one night when their building's old furnace was rattling in protest against the cold while Andy Williams was crooning "It's the most wonderful time of the year" on the kitchen radio, she snapped.

"Oh stuff it," Kathy yelled at Williams. It didn't matter that it was only the radio, and Williams had died in 2012.

Her son looked up at her from the kitchen table, questioningly.

"I think I'm coming down with a cold," she said to explain away her bad mood.

Christmas morning was rainy and overcast, but Luke's smile was as bright as a Caribbean beach at noon when he tore open the wrapping paper and opened the box to reveal his new jacket.

"Oh boy! Thanks, Mom! Cool! It's just what I wanted!" he said.

"It's from Grandma and me," Kathy noted, happier than she'd been in a long time. Seeing Luke's grin made all those long shifts worth it.

"Try it on!" she prompted.

It fit fine, with a little room for his always-expanding length.

Luke wore the jacket proudly every day. He watched the Colts get to the playoffs, and then be beaten by one lousy field goal. But he never wavered in his support, and the jacket truly was his prized possession.

One day in February, however, he came home from school without it.

"Where is your coat?" Kathy asked sharply, since it was sub-zero outside.

"I gave it to Barry, because he didn't have a coat," Luke replied. "All he had to wear outside this winter was a hoodie."

"You gave it to Barry?" Kathy repeated, dumbfounded.

"Yeah, Mom; it's better to give than to receive, you know, and you should love your enemies," Luke said matter-of-factly. "I can wear my old coat."

Christmas came about two months late to Kathy that year, but Luke gave her a wonderful gift.

She knew that despite their problems, with a son like that they'd be just fine.

2

Yes, Amanda, There Is a Tree

Roger Markowitz knew all the tunnels under New York City's Rockefeller Center. He had scouted them out in the five years he'd worked as an auditor for Deloitte & Touche at 30 Rock.

But this evening he had to venture above ground to hail a cab. He had a meeting across town at his club, which made it impossible to avoid the tourists in Manhattan to see THE TREE.

New York was a prime destination for those who celebrate Christmas, and the huge Rockefeller Center Christmas tree screwed up his life annually. It seemed like the whole world made a pilgrimage to see its thousands of lights each year.

Roger didn't understand all the fuss. He was Jewish, although he avoided practicing his faith almost as diligently as he avoided tourists.

He had to walk several blocks to have any hope of finding a cab. But there were tourists here too. About a dozen college co-eds who were in town for a good time were headed straight for him, thoroughly blocking the sidewalk.

They weren't much younger than he was, but they seemed to be geographically challenged.

"Excuse me, which way to the tree?" a brunette with bright green eyes asked him politely.

"Tree? There is no tree this year," replied Roger, straightening the black cashmere scarf under his heavy black trench coat.

The girls looked even more confused.

"But I'm sure there is," the brunette said. "If there wasn't, we would have heard about it."

"Go two blocks straight ahead, turn left, and follow the crowd," Roger growled, relenting.

The girls gave him a puzzled look and a quick "Thanks!" and sauntered away.

"Damn tourists," Roger muttered under his breath. He turned up the collar on his coat so it protected the back of his neck and the bottom of his medium-brown hair.

Traffic was always bad, and the added excursion buses belching black smoke and sitting curbside as their passengers got on or off didn't help.

It was bad enough that there were so many extra people in the city this time of year, but their behavior annoyed him.

All these people were gawkers.

Roger was accustomed to walking with his head almost down in order to avoid the gaze of panhandlers and pickpockets. In contrast, the tourists looked up as much as they looked ahead. It was like they'd never seen a skyscraper.

The ones that linked arms and walked seven abreast on the sidewalk for protection from God knows what irked him the most. They made it impossible to pass.

Roger had never liked crowds, which was strange for a man who was born and raised in Manhattan.

He was an only child, but he was never "close" with his parents. They'd moved to a condo in Fort Lauderdale, Florida a few years ago, and he hadn't seen them in over a year.

He usually worked over the Christmas holiday, trying his best to get the year-end reports in order. Besides tax time, it was his most stressful time of the year.

But this year things were going remarkably smoothly. The new computer system that almost caused everyone in his department to be fired last year was now doing what it had been designed to do, with only a few exceptions. For the first time since he'd joined the company, Roger's department was getting a Christmas vacation, and he was determined to make the most of it.

He paid through the nose when he made his flights online due to the late booking, but Roger was headed to Cancun for the holidays. He planned to sit in the sun poolside and drink margaritas all Christmas Day. And with a little luck like he'd enjoyed there in the past, he'd have mindless but mind-blowing sex with some long-legged beauty on New Year's Eve.

He would have just enough time to pack before heading to LaGuardia for tomorrow morning's flight.

He wasn't able to book his customary first-class seat due to the late booking, so Roger was with the rest of the herd in the boarding area as the different groups were called the following day. When he reached his aisle seat near the back of the plane, he was surprised to see a mother in the window seat and a young girl in the middle.

The girl looked to be about 6, and she was dressed in a pink and purple Halloween costume. She was wearing black patent-leather shoes and pink ankle socks with white ruffles around the edges. Pink tights peeked out under her costume. She was wearing pink lipstick too, but most of it slid to the bottom right-hand side of her cheek as she wiped her mouth with the back of her hand.

Roger wasn't sure, but he thought she was supposed to be a fairy, as she had white and silver wings on her back that poked out into the adjoining seats. Her mother was trying to get her to take her wings off, but the girl wasn't budging.

"Amanda, you really must take off your wings for the flight," said her mother, a blonde who looked to be about the same age as Roger.

"No! I won't!" Amanda pouted with a tap of one shoe, narrowly missing Roger's left calf.

At that point the flight attendant intervened. After some convincing, Amanda's wings were carefully placed in the overhead bin in exchange for some costume jewelry in the shape of wings that the flight attendant produced.

Roger took out his reading glasses, opened the business section of his newspaper, and hoped that was the end of the drama.

"My name is Amanda. What's yours?" the little girl asked, looking up at Roger.

She was young, so Roger tried to be nice.

"Roger," was his one-word reply.

"Roger, like in just Roger, or Roger, like in over and out?" Amanda wanted to know.

"I'm sorry; she'll talk your ears off," Amanda's mother apologized.

Roger shot her a weak smile.

"My name is Roger," he explained.

"Very pleased to meet you, Roger," Amanda said with great politeness. "My name is Amanda O'Leary. I'm 5 and a half. Mommy let me wear some of her pink lipstick!"

Roger nodded, hoping that was the end of it.

It wasn't.

"We were visiting Grandma and Grandpa in Brooklyn!" Amanda explained. "And we all went into 'Hattan and saw the big Christmas tree! It was be-U-ti-ful!" she pronounced.

"Ah yes, the tree," was all Roger said in reply, but Amanda was just getting started.

"We went ice skating on the pond there, and I only fell about five times!" she reported, referring, Roger guessed, to the ice skating rink in front of the tree.

"Grandpa held me up. And we ate lunch in a fancy restaurant with white napkins and pretty china and there were angels! And we saw some be-U-ti-ful store windows, and we got to ride in a carriage! The horse was brown, and his name was Joe. And we saw a big snowflake, and a store that was wrapped in a big red ribbon!"

Roger looked like a deer caught in headlights.

"I'm very sorry," Amanda's mother repeated. "She's a little excited."

Roger didn't want to be around if she was ever more than a little excited.

"My daddy and Stevie are sitting up front; we couldn't get seats together," Amanda continued in another long rush of words, her little hand vaguely pointing to the front of the plane.

Then she switched back to her previous topic without warning.

"And there were a lot of people everywhere, and we got to see the kets!"

Roger looked at Amanda's mother, mystified.

"We saw the Rockettes at Radio City Music Hall," Amanda's mother explained.

"And Mary and Joseph were there, and Baby Jesus, and a real donkey, and real camels!" Amanda continued.

"Ah, very nice," Roger said as he turned a page of his newspaper and hoped Amanda would take a hint.

Amanda was oblivious to it, but interested in Roger.

"Why are you reading the paper? Are you going to the beach? Do you have any boys and girls?" she asked in one breath.

"Um, no," Roger said, choosing to answer the last question asked.

"We are!" Amanda informed him triumphantly, referring to question number two in the string.

"Very nice," Roger repeated. She was tiring, but he had to admit she was cute.

He decided to be nice.

"What did you like best about your visit to New York, Amanda?" he asked.

"Oh, the tree," she said firmly, without missing a beat.

Amanda squeezed the armrests tightly when the plane took off; her little feet didn't hit the floor. Once they were airborne, she focused her attention on the scene outside the window.

But when the clouds obstructed her view, her focus returned to Roger.

"Do you have any little boys and girls?" she asked him again.

"Ah, no, I'm not married," Roger replied.

"Well, why not?" Amanda demanded.

"I guess I haven't found the right one yet," Roger said quietly.

"Well what are you waiting for?" Amanda asked, as her mother looked at Roger apologetically. "There are lots of nice ladies around. Maybe you could marry my teacher, Mrs. Buck. She's very nice!

"Oh, but Mrs. Buck is already married," Amanda corrected herself, which sent her into a fit of giggles. "That wouldn't work I guess! You know what, Roger?"

Roger was afraid to respond, even if he would have been able to get a word in edgewise.

"I'm going to be a big sister! Mommy has a baby boy or a baby girl in her tummy right now!"

"Amanda!" her mother said sharply, shocked. "Sit still, be quiet, and play with your iPad."

With a sigh Amanda turned her attention to the iPad, but the drone of the plane's engines and the gentle motion of the plane soon lulled her to sleep. As she slept her right hand was gently hooked in the crook of Roger's left arm. Her little lips were still open, although gratefully they were finally quiet.

Amanda's mother started to move her daughter, but Roger motioned for her to let her sleep.

Amanda's chubby little fingers felt good resting on his arm.

Amanda slept for the rest of the flight, only awaking when the plane's wheels touched the warm tarmac in Mexico.

At that point there was a flurry of activity to make sure nothing was left on board as they departed. Roger let Amanda and her mother go ahead of him down the aisle of the plane.

"Goodbye, Roger," Amanda said formally as she turned to take her mother's hand. "Maybe we'll see you on the beach!"

"Maybe you will; goodbye, Amanda," Roger said. "It's been, ah, memorable."

Roger did sit in the sun poolside at his hotel in Cancun on Christmas Day, drinking margaritas and thinking about what he wanted in life.

He did the same thing the day after Christmas as he began to realize that a 5-year-old, brown-eyed casual acquaintance dressed like a sugar-plum fairy had been a profound influence on his life.

Two days after Christmas he faced the fact that he wanted to make some big changes.

Instead of trolling the bar on New Year's Eve in search of some meaningless sex, he was on a flight to Fort Lauderdale to visit his parents, a changed man.

He wasn't sure if a child of his own would ever be in the cards or not, but Amanda O'Leary had definitely taught him a little about Christmas and a lot about tolerance towards those holiday revelers around Rockefeller Center's Christmas tree.

3

'Ouch!' Said the Donkey, All Shaggy and Brown

Josh Martin could hardly contain himself.

Santa was coming tonight, but before that Josh was going to be an acolyte at church for the very first time!

Pastor Simmons and Mr. Schilling, the head usher, had given him his instructions after church last Sunday.

Mr. Schilling made him promise not to chew gum, make sure his longish-brown hair was combed, wear regular loafers instead of his sneakers, and not to hurry when he walked down the aisle. He was supposed to keep his head up and his eyes straight ahead too.

Mr. Schilling would help him put on the acolyte's bright red robe in the church basement at 6:30 p.m. That's when he'd get the candle-lighter too. The handle on the candlelighter that made the taper go up and down stuck a little, but Josh thought it would be OK.

Mr. Schilling would light the taper at the back of the church at the stroke of 7 p.m., and then Josh would lead the kids' choir down the big aisle in the middle of the church. Pews full of people would flank both sides of the aisle, as the Christmas Eve service was usually standing room only.

A pregnant Mary would follow the kids' choir. That was really Marti Cook with a pillow tied around her waist. She'd wear her bathrobe, and she'd have a towel on her head as a scarf. Marti was Josh's babysitter sometimes. Everyone — especially Matt Stine — thought she was pretty.

Matt, who was the star pitcher for the Chapel Hill Hornets, would play Joseph. He'd be in a bathrobe too, and both Matt and Marti would wear sandals. Matt would carry one of his brother Bob's ski poles as a staff.

The grown-up choir would follow Mary and Joseph down the aisle. Three kids dressed as wise men and a bunch of other kids dressed as shepherds and angels would join Mary and Joseph a little later, during their annual Living Nativity skit.

The Humphreys' new baby would be Jesus, even though she was really a girl. Josh thought that was lame, but in a small town like Chapel Hill you had to make do sometimes.

The older kids in the church's youth group and some adults had made a new set for the skit this year, and Josh and all the other kids thought it was cool. There was an outline of a stable, a manger of course, and a life-size cow and donkey made out of paper mache over wire foundations. The manger was full of real straw, and there was even a fake, brown-and-green palm tree and a big, silver paper mache star overhead.

The cow was a little lopsided and a bit cross-eyed, but the donkey had turned out great. He was painted light brown, like milky coffee. He had big blue marbles for eyes. His mane, tail, and eyelashes were made out of heavy rope that was frayed just right. With his long eyelashes, at first glance it looked like he was flirting with the cow.

When Josh got up to the altar, he was to bow at the big gold cross in the center of the altar and then light the two big, white altar candles, starting with the one on the right. He had to be careful not to let any wax drip. When that mission was accomplished, he was to go over to the acolyte's chair, which was between the altar and the stable, and sit down. He was supposed to try hard to sit up straight and not to fidget during the rest of the service.

This was a big night, however, and he still had one more huge duty.

Josh was to start the whole skit off by lighting the big white Christ candle on the advent wreath, which was right beside the stable. He'd light the four big blue advent candles right after that, and Pastor Simmons would say a special prayer before the skit started.

Mr. Schilling said all the candles could remain lit throughout the service. They'd snuff them out together after everything was over.

Josh could hardly wait!

Josh walked slowly down the aisle at the stroke of 7, and his parents beamed with pride from their seats on the right-hand side of the church. He forgot to bow at the cross, but he lit the two big altar candles with no problems. The red robe was a bit scratchy around the neckline, and he squirmed a little during the reading of the first lesson, but hardly anyone noticed.

The kids' choir sang "The Friendly Beasts" with much enthusiasm, if not perfect pitch, and soon it was time for Josh to light the advent wreath.

He carefully lit the Christ candle, just as he'd been told. He thought the fourth and final blue candle might go out right after he lit it, but a second later it was burning as brightly as the others.

Relieved, Josh pushed the little handle to pull the taper back down the candlelighter. In his excitement he pushed the wrong way and too hard, and the brand-new taper extended all the way out.

Suddenly it was like he was holding a burning fishing pole!

Before he could move the handle the other way, a spark hit a tiny clump of dry straw next to the manger. As Josh, the Holy Family, and the entire congregation looked on in shock, the straw flamed up and ignited the donkey's rope tail. It went up in flames as quickly as the fireworks at Chapel Hill Park on the Fourth of July, igniting a light blue banner that one of the women's circles had sewn as a decoration for that side of the sanctuary. It read "I bring GOOD NEWS for ALL PEOPLE" in big black letters, but the royal blue edging on the right side was now ablaze with yellow flames.

Mary and Joseph's mouths dropped open. Being a perceptive baby and Lord of all, Jesus began to wail. Josh wanted to sink into a hole in the floor, but his new black loafers seemed to be glued to the carpet. Pastor Simmons' eyes got as big as saucers, but he was immobile too.

Finally Rusty Souder and Danny Harris, who were both members of Chapel Hill's volunteer fire company, sprang into action. As Jesus continued to cry, they stomped at the flames they could reach with their feet. Rusty then ran to the side of the church for a fire extinguisher mounted on the wall; quickly returned, and sprayed the entire Living Nativity with a layer of sticky white foam.

The church was quiet after the hisses of the extinguisher were over, except Baby Jesus was still crying uncontrollably. Mary brushed foam from her face with the towel that she'd been using as a headscarf. Joseph ducked right before the big, silver star that had been on top of the stable would have hit him on the head.

Mrs. McAllister, the organist, came to terms with what had happened first. When she saw the danger was over, she belted out the first song she could think of on the organ, which was "We Wish You a Merry Christmas."

Pastor Simmons may have missed his calling. He could have been an actor, because his face registered almost every emotion known to man until he settled on a little smile that quickly erupted into an uncontrolled fit of the giggles.

Mr. Schilling wasn't smiling, but he and the two volunteer firefighters moved among the cast of the Living Nativity to make sure everyone was OK. Mrs. Humphrey rushed up front, took her baby from Mary, and quickly quieted her. Order began to be restored.

Pastor Simmons' face was bright red, and he was still smiling when he addressed the congregation.

"In light of the recent occurrences, let's all carefully continue with the candlelighting and singing of 'Silent Night' to conclude our services," he said.

In one motion the congregation quickly reached for the individual candles they had received before they entered the sanctuary, and Mrs. McAllister ran through an introduction of "Silent Night" very quietly. She then stalled for time with a quiet version of "Hark the Herald Angels Sing" when she — and everyone else — realized there was no acolyte to light the ushers' candles. Josh had moved back to the acolyte's chair sometime during the melee, but his head was down, his shoulders were heaving, and he was crying quietly.

Pastor Simmons patted Josh on the back and whispered to him that everything was going to be fine. Josh wasn't convinced. His tears abated a bit, but his head was still down. As far as he was concerned, Christmas, if not his entire life, was over.

Mr. Schilling couldn't find his matches, and at first no one else seemed to have any either. Chapel Hill had adopted a "no smoking in public places" policy during the election two years ago, and even the people who smoked didn't seem to have any matches on them at church. Finally two old guys from the VFW produced one set of matches and a lime green Bic lighter, and the ushers started to make their way through the congregation to light the candle of the first person in each row.

The church looked as beautiful as it did every Christmas as the overhead lights were turned off, and only the flames of the parishioners' small candles illuminated the sanctuary. Mrs. McAllister turned up the volume on "Silent Night," and everyone was smiling by verse two.

Santa still came to Josh Martin's house later that night.

The women in the ladies' circle sewed a new banner, and the youth group made the donkey a new tail.

Josh grew up to become an insurance agent, and still lives in town today.

Even though he has kids of his own now, Josh still can't think of that night without cringing.

Everyone else says it was the best Christmas Eve service ever held at Chapel Hill Baptist Church.

It's quietly referred to as the "Christmas Eve of the Flaming Ass" throughout the Midwest.

4

No Hunting Allowed

Deb Brady paused her vacuum cleaner, stuck her finger in the mini blind of her living room's picture window, and tried to get a better look at her neighbor across the street.

For families of a similar economic background living in semi-posh Tarrington Estates outside of Louisville, Kentucky, the Bradys and the Mitchells couldn't be more different.

Deb Brady and her husband Brad both worked for an accounting firm in downtown Louisville. They had two teenage daughters who were both in contention for college tennis scholarships. The entire family was vegan. They spent their summers on the family sailboat; they were members of the local country club, and they were all active runners. Their home was a trim, traditional two-story colonial with white siding, black shutters, and lovely rose gardens that were Deb's pride and joy.

Mike Mitchell, who lived in a rambling but a bit shabby brick ranch across the street, had been a plumber all his adult life. He was divorced and the father of two teenage sons, neither of which wanted to do any work at all. They were coasting through high school, and their primary hobbies were playing video games and pool.

The entire family liked to hunt and fish, and they were all card-carrying members of the NRA. They were also known to tip back a few too many beers at loud parties they occasionally hosted around a campfire in their back yard before and after hunting trips.

The Mitchells owned two hunting dogs. One was a big black Lab mix named Duke. The other was primarily of German Shepherd ancestry who answered to the name of Lug.

The Bradys' main strategy in interacting with the Mitchells was to ignore them as much as possible, which was fine with the Mitchells, and for the most part it was successful. The Bradys thought the Mitchells were rednecks and the Mitchells felt the Bradys were snooty. It wasn't a cold war, exactly, but it was definitely chilly.

Their first interaction came shortly after the Mitchells moved in, about three years ago. Deb caught Lug right after he dug up four peony bushes she had just planted in front of her back picket fence. When she confronted Mike about it he said it couldn't have been his dog, because his dogs never left his property without him.

Their last interaction had come about a year ago, when Deb called the homeowners' association to complain about the freshly-killed buck hanging in the Mitchells' carport, as they bled it out before butchering. Deb didn't know exactly what her representative said, but the buck was gone the following day.

She hadn't been as successful in other complaints about the smoke drifting from the Mitchells' campfires onto her property. The camp-fires, often unattended, continued most weekends throughout the year. They were always accompanied by country music from a boom box or two, played so loudly it drowned out the jazz playing from the Bradys' own sound system on their back patio.

Deb didn't have a clear view of what Mike was working on this December morning, but a bright yellow extension ladder was leaning beside the old oak tree next to his carport.

Maybe he's getting ready to hang himself Deb thought, and then was immediately ashamed of herself.

He's probably just putting up his Christmas decorations she thought with more charity.

The Mitchells' Christmas lawn decorations consisted of huge inflatables purchased at the local home-improvement store. They added to their collection annually with whatever was marked down after Christmas. The balloons were colorful and quite big when inflated. Deb knew these decorations were popular, but there seemed to be problems with the blowers because mostly they were just deflated puddles of nylon lying in various spots throughout the Mitchells' lawn.

Her own outdoor decorations had been installed last weekend. She always went for an understated, elegant look, and she was excited about her addition to this year's display.

On a family trip to Gatlinburg, Tennessee, in the fall she had stumbled upon a woodcrafter offering outdoor decorations of almost full-size reindeer made out of driftwood. She purchased nine of them for the lawn to the left of the pergola that covered her Grecian urn water feature.

Some of the deer sculptures had antlers and some did not. Some were standing and some were down on all fours, nestled in the light dusting of snow that had fallen two days ago. At the back of the display she had placed two deer with antlers who were on their hind legs as if they were playing. Tiny white lights were interspersed throughout each of the nine reindeer, giving them a mystical look. The reindeer closest to the house sported a bit of red paint on his snout, signifying that he was Rudolph.

Deb had a knack of arranging anything, whether it was flowers, furniture, her family's social calendar, or these reindeer. She was secretly hoping her outdoor Christmas decorations would be included on the list of outstanding residential Christmas displays to visit that was published annually in her local garden club's newsletter.

But all hopes for that were dashed when she saw the Mitchells' finished display.

Mike had erected a tree stand in his oak tree. A huge nylon, inflated Santa in camouflage gear was on the stand, leaning against a large branch of the oak tree. He was holding an inflated rifle pointed directly at the Brady family's new reindeer.

He's gone too far again! Deb thought angrily. *Not only is that not nice, what message is it for the neighborhood kids?*

Less than 5 minutes later she was leaving a voicemail on the cell phone of her homeowner association's representative.

When he called her back an hour later, she was not pleased with the result.

"I don't think there's much I can do about it, Deb," said Harry McCombs. "There are definite rules in the homeowner association's bylaws about animals in the development, both living and dead, but this is just a Christmas decoration on his own property."

"Well, if you're not going to help me, then I'll find someone else who will," she vowed.

Her husband, Brad, could see the situation plainly when he returned home from the country club. It was hard to miss. He knew his wife would be upset. He also wasn't surprised when he learned of the homeowner association representative's reaction.

"I think this is in direct retaliation from our previous complaint," he told his steaming wife. "I'll try to talk to the Mitchells calmly about it, but don't hold your breath."

The next afternoon, right after church, Brad knocked on the Mitchells' door.

He was cordial; there was no doubt about it.

"Hi Mike; Merry Christmas!" Brad began.

"Merry Christmas to you," Mike replied.

"I was wondering if I could talk to you about your Christmas display," Brad asked. "I'm sure you'll admit it's pretty unconventional. I was wondering if you would take it down, just so it doesn't give the wrong message to the kids."

"Well, Brad, is it?" Mike responded. "We like our display, and we want to keep it up. We think most kids will know it's just a joke."

Brad decided to level with him.

"I'm sorry, Mike, but it upsets my wife," he replied. "We're vegans, and the gun is pointed right at our reindeer display. I'm asking you again, nicely, to take it down."

"Well I'm sorry, Brad, but it's staying up," Mike said with conviction. "It's just a joke, and we all think it's a pretty funny one. Tell your wife to relax and not get her panties in a wad over it."

Realizing he was getting nowhere, Brad said goodbye and left before someone turned a gun on him.

Deb was not happy with his results.

To her credit, she slept on the problem overnight, but she dialed her friend Anne at the local newspaper the next morning, as well as the news desks of all four local TV stations.

And all five media outlets covered the story. They told her side of the story clearly, and they all got a comment from Mike as well.

"It's just a joke!" he insisted on air, in print, and to anyone else who asked.

Deb did get her wish about her Christmas display being listed in her garden club's newsletter, but unfortunately the Mitchells' display was photographed alongside her reindeer. That happened in the newspaper as well, and with the TV coverage to boot soon there was a steady stream of cars turning up their street to look at the now-famous displays. Both families were kept awake into the wee hours each night as the cars' headlights bounced into their bedroom windows when the drivers turned around at the end of the cul-de-sac.

Mike kept his display's blowers going constantly, so there was no hope of it deflating prematurely.

After a suggestion planted by Deb, two local elementary schools sent handmade Christmas cards to the Mitchells asking them to not shoot Rudolph and to take Santa the Hunter down. Another neighbor made a video of the standoff that went viral and was picked up by all the national morning and late-night TV shows.

Both Deb and Mike got more stubborn as Christmas approached, with no solution in sight.

But on Dec. 22 an unlikely ally turned the tables in Deb's favor.

Lug got loose that morning, went tearing after a rabbit, and bounced into the Bradys' garden as he ran after the bunny. Deb saw him from the back door and worked quickly, luring him into their garage with a waffle she'd just made for Brad's breakfast. After devouring it in four bites, Lug would have followed her anywhere.

Lug was in no danger in the Bradys' garage. As it turned out, he was the happiest kidnapping victim in the history of crime.

Deb went to the grocery store and bought him a far more expensive dog food than he was accustomed to. She made sure he had plenty of fresh water, and she made a bed for him out of an old sleeping bag. She lavished him with attention, gave him a few toys, and offered him the biggest rawhide bone her grocery store sold. She took him behind the garage regularly to do his business, making sure they weren't seen.

Then she contemplated her next move from this vastly improved strategic position.

This time she wasn't leaving it up to her husband.

She decided to wait a day to be sure Lug was missed. The next evening she marched over to the Mitchells' back door and knocked.

Mike came almost at once, although he was definitely surprised to see who was calling.

"Hello, Mike," Deb began, pleasantly. "You know that we'd all like you to take your Christmas display down, immediately," she said. "And I'd like you to know that my underwear is definitely laying smoothly. I'd also like you to know that one of your dogs that you say never goes off your property, has indeed gone off your property, and is now sitting in my garage chewing on a big rawhide bone. I'll give him back to you right now if you agree to take your Santa down."

Mike, who had secretly been hoping for a graceful way out after receiving the Christmas cards from the elementary school children, finally relented.

"Well Deb, I guess you got me," he said. "Let's go get Lug, and maybe we can also go get a beer."

A couple of hours later a slightly more-loose Deb agreed to let bygones be bygones. Mike took Santa the Hunter down the next day, and happiness and peace returned to the Tarrington Estates subdivision in time for Christmas.

5

And Goodwill to All Men

Minerva Stewart made the best apple pie in all of Cumberland County; maybe even in all of Pennsylvania.

It wasn't a boast.

It was fact.

She'd made at least a dozen apple pies for the annual Christmas Bazaar at Sunnyside Methodist Church every year since she was 15.

She turned 79 in July, so that was at least 880 apple pies.

Due to high demand, her contributions were never displayed with the other baked goods in the church's Fellowship Hall. Minerva's pies were always pre-ordered through a sign-up sheet posted outside the church office the Sunday before the bazaar. Each year, all 12 pies were spoken for before the choir walked down the aisle to begin the 10:30 a.m. service.

It had always been that way. Tradition, you see, was important at Sunnyside Methodist Church.

So this Saturday morning, Minerva scurried around her kitchen preparing the ingredients for the recipe she — and only she — knew by heart.

Once she had agreed to let her 12-year-old granddaughter, Wanda, watch her bake, because Wanda wanted to follow in her grandmother's footsteps, at least in the kitchen. Wanda tried to intercept the ingredients and measure them before they went into Minerva's big blue mixing bowl, but the effort was a dismal failure because Minerva never measured anything. She simply poured this and that into her concoction, spread out her crust on a large marble slab that had been HER grandmother's, and the pies emerged from the gas oven an hour later as delicious as they'd always been.

Nobody ever thought this would change, least of all Minerva.

The crust for the first round of pies came out flaky and buttery, and Minerva was ready to mix the main ingredients for the filling — which included both white and brown sugar — when the phone rang. It was Judy Wilson, who had known Minerva all her life. She asked Minerva to bring some big spoons to church for the bazaar. They always needed more spoons when serving lunch out of the big crockpots at the lunch stand.

Minerva readily agreed and then went back to her baking, humming a Christmas carol as she worked. She had to make the pies in three different batches, because although her oven was big, it could only hold four pies at a time.

When the first four pies came out of the oven they looked a little different than usual, but Minerva failed to realize that she'd omitted the white sugar after she was distracted by Judy's phone call.

The second round of pies seemed much better, although Minerva forgot to add the lemon zest after she stopped for a spot of tea.

The third batch was the most troubling. Although she'd focused solely on the task at hand, Minerva somehow forgot to add almost half of the required all-purpose flour.

Oh, they'll be OK; they're always OK Minerva thought as she put the last four pies on the table in the sunporch to cool.

After another cup of tea, Minerva was ready for her next task. This one was harder, but she wanted to do it in honor of her husband, Ralph, who had died unexpectedly in February of a heart attack.

For years Ralph had put a Christmas display on their barn's tallest silo. Since the farm was situated at the top of one of the biggest hills in the county, the display could be seen for miles in the rolling countryside.

It, too, was tradition.

So Minerva bundled up in her work jacket and jammed Ralph's favorite red-plaid cap over her tight, gray curls. She pulled on her gloves, tucked a scarf under her jacket, and trundled out to the steer barn to get the big ladder that waited in the cobwebs behind the heavy, sliding double door. The display, which came in three sections, would be waiting in the hayloft just above the door.

Minerva found the ladder. The three wire forms covered in fake pine garland and lights were where they were supposed to be. She positioned the ladder against the side of the silo, tried not to think about how high she had to climb, and started up.

The first tricky part was maneuvering from her ladder onto the bottom of the metal ladder that was attached to the side of the silo. Minerva took a deep breath and stepped onto the bottom of the silo's ladder, holding all three sections of the display in her right hand as she clung to the ladder with her left hand.

She climbed and climbed, and then she climbed some more. It took awhile because it was a 200-foot silo, and the nails for the display were about halfway up.

She passed the bottom set of nails for the third section of the display, and she was relieved that they were holding firm in the concrete.

She passed the second set of nails without snagging her clothing on them, and she was quite proud about how things were going. It was hard, but everyone she knew enjoyed this display every Christmas, and she couldn't let them down.

She held on tight to the ladder with one hand and settled the first section of the display over its nails. She almost cheered when it was straight on the first try.

The second section was a little harder, and she felt a little dizzy once, but she got it up too.

That's when she noticed the big black steer looking up at her.

"Why hello there!" she yelled down to the steer. "What are you looking at?"

It never occurred to her that the sight of a 79-year-old woman hanging with one hand onto the side of a concrete silo more than 100 feet up in the air would be awe-inspiring to all creatures, including a cow.

Minerva wondered which steer it was. There were only a few left on the farm, but she'd known most of them since they were calves, and she had given them all names.

Unfortunately the distraction of the steer was enough to cause her to forget to connect the electrical plugs of the second and third sections of the display. In her effort to keep her balance, she didn't realize the mistake.

The third section installed, she slowly made her way back down the silo's ladder. She was pleased to see that her first ladder hadn't shifted from where she'd left it. She slowly made the transition and was quite pleased with herself when she plugged in the electrical cord and set the timer for the display to come on promptly at 7 p.m.

How's that, Michael? she thought smugly. Michael was her only son, and Wanda's father. They'd had words right after Ralph died when he first suggested that she sell the farm and move into a condo down by the river. They'd had an actual argument when he nagged her about it again at Thanksgiving. She knew Christmas wouldn't stop his crusade, but she wasn't ready to move off the farm yet.

About three days after the bazaar the hushed conversations started, after the pie purchasers partook of their desserts.

It was downright shocking to even suggest it, but the truth was this year Minerva's pies were not quite right.

Was anything the matter with Minerva?

As Minerva's long-time friend, Judy was appointed to broach the subject.

"Minerva dear, did you do anything differently with your apple pies for the bazaar this year?" Judy began.

"No, they were the same as always," Minerva said.

"Are you sure you didn't change the recipe?" Judy pressed on.

"Recipe? There is no recipe," Minerva replied. "Is everything OK?"

"Well, some of the people mentioned that they tasted a little different," Judy said.

"Different? Well, I didn't do anything different," Minerva responded, and Judy dropped the subject, afraid of upsetting her old friend.

Michael dropped Minerva off at church at 6 p.m. on Christmas Eve. She was an hour early, but she wanted to beat the crowd and "get there early so I can get a good seat in the back."

The service went as expected, as was the tradition at Sunnyside Methodist Church. The old Christmas carols were sung, some babies were taken out of the sanctuary halfway through the service when they started to cry, and the kids' choir was as cute as ever. Most of the congregation stuck with the preacher's message until at least halfway through the sermon, which was also par for the course.

Despite the beauty of the service, Minerva was still mad at her son as the ushers started down the aisles to light the candle held by the first person in each pew. Honestly, she thought he was more of an old lady than she would ever be.

It's not that I couldn't be happy in town, but it's just not time yet, Minerva thought. *I can still do things, even if my pies were a flop this year.*

The ushers slowly made their way towards the back of the church. As Minerva took the flame from her son's candle to light her own, the sad look in Michael's eyes spoke volumes. Minerva knew he didn't want to spoil her Christmas. He must really be worried about her to make such a fuss.

Living in town might not be so bad, she thought. *I do have a lot to take care of each day at the farm. I don't want to move, but I also don't want to cause trouble, especially at Christmas.*

On the way home in the darkened SUV, she carefully broached the subject.

"It might not be so bad to move into town," she said hesitantly. "Judy has a condo there, and she loves it."

"Judy is in a club that plays rummy every Tuesday at the community center," Michael pointed out. "I think you could beat them all."

"I'm sure I could," Minerva said confidently. "I can still get things done."

As the car made the turn up the lane towards the farmhouse, the Christmas lights on the silo glowed their message over the rolling fields. Michael was astonished to see them, and a stab of pure fear went up his spine as it dawned on him who put them up.

"PEACE" the top section proclaimed.

The words "ON EARTH" couldn't be seen, since their plugs had been left dangling on high.

"You sure can, Mom," Michael replied.

6

North-Bound and Down

Jim pulled the tractor-trailer off I-75 and onto the entrance ramp for the rest stop in Tennessee. Although he liked driving when the highway was deserted, he was more than ready to call it a night.

He'd been driving the 18-wheeler all day, hauling a load of cantaloupe he'd picked up near Pensacola, Florida. He was scheduled to deliver it to a distribution center in Michigan tomorrow, which just happened to be Christmas Day. The trucking company that he worked for tried its best to get each driver home for Christmas, but the dispatcher was in a pinch this year, and Jim had agreed to make the run. It was no big deal. He'd be home in Ohio with his wife, Chris, for the big family get-together on the 26th.

After he prepared the truck and its delicate contents for the night and made the proper notations in his logbook, Jim headed for the restroom and washed up. He'd sleep in his truck tonight. Its sleeping berth was small but it wasn't bad since he'd purchased a new foam mattress for it in the spring at a discount store in Georgia.

All it was missing was Chris.

It was the second marriage for both of them, but he'd finally found his soulmate. She hardly ever complained about him being away from home so much. She was left to handle a lot of things he should be doing, but she usually took it in stride. And she made his house a home.

She'd welcomed the two children from his first marriage — who were grown up now — unconditionally. She got worked up when she was feeding a crowd like she'd be doing two days from now, but she always pulled it off like she was some country version of Martha Stewart.

Jim remembered how lost he'd been when his first marriage disintegrated, and thanked the big man upstairs for hooking him up with Chris about a year later.

That was eight years ago now.

He'd never been so scared as he was when Chris was diagnosed with breast cancer. She had a complete mastectomy followed by chemo and radiation, but she'd been cancer-free for two years now and he thanked God for that every single day.

Jim wasn't a churchgoer, but Chris enjoyed church. He went with her now and then just to make her happy, but as he pointed out to her, even Jesus wasn't a regular churchgoer. In the Bible he just visited the temple a couple of times.

Chris loved Christmas. She watched the family budget judiciously, and purchased Christmas presents throughout the year when things went on sale.

That was the direct opposite of his approach. Each year he purchased the $50 gift cards he needed at a truck stop about a week before Christmas. His Christmas shopping took about 15 minutes. No wrapping paper was involved because he dropped each gift card into a Christmas card, signed his and Chris's names, and was done.

The only present he had struggled with was the one for Chris, but a few years into their marriage they decided to skip gifts for each other and concentrate on the kids.

As Jim left the rest stop's building that housed the restrooms, the moon glistened off the snow that blanketed the ground. The rest stop was deserted; most people were already home with their families. He could hear some traffic and see some lights on the interstate occasionally, but it was unusually quiet.

Jim had stopped at this rest area many times in the past, so he knew the layout. There was a spot for people to walk their dogs to the left of the main building. On the right were picnic tables overlooking a spectacular view of the valley.

Jim zipped up his new, tan jacket and pulled its hood over his camouflage cap. He was glad he had gloves in his jacket pocket, and he put them on.

Man; it's cold here in the woods! he thought.

Although he was tired he wasn't quite ready to sleep yet, so he brushed the snow off the top of one of the picnic tables and climbed up, his feet resting on the bench.

The valley spread out in front of him, giving him an amazing view. It was like being in a small plane, only better because the field of vision was larger. Lights from various small Tennessee towns dotted the landscape, but it was the moon and the stars that were truly spectacular.

It was so quiet. The only sound he heard was his own breath as he exhaled and made a tiny vapor trail in the crisp winter air.

The smell of pine emanated from the nearby forest. It was more pungent than anyone's live Christmas tree.

He bet there were plenty of deer in the woods rimming the picnic area. Maybe a couple of them were looking at him.

Chris would be almost finished at church about now. He'd wait until he was back in the truck before he gave her a call. One of the reasons he stopped at this particular rest area was because he knew it had good cell phone reception. If it wasn't so dark, you could even see the tower over by the dog-walking area.

It sure was a lonely place to be on Christmas Eve.

Funny that he didn't feel lonely at all.

This is my kind of church he thought.

His thoughts drifted to the familiar story he'd known since he was a child.

Jim liked the part about the shepherds the best. They were wanderers with a job to do, just like him.

The story said that the shepherds were terrified when the angels showed up. No kidding! Jim would have shit his pants if he saw an actual angel.

Jim wondered if he would have done the right thing if he had been one of those shepherds. Would he have left his flocks and headed into Bethlehem like they did, to try to find some baby in a stable?

Or would he have just laughed it off, and thought he'd gotten some bad booze somewhere?

He had to hand it to those shepherds. They not only checked things out, but they also told everybody they met about Jesus afterwards.

"Actually, they were the first disciples," Jim said aloud, surprising himself.

The stars are bright tonight! he thought. *I wonder if the shepherds were looking up at these same stars before the angels appeared to them that night?*

As if in answer to his question, he spotted a shooting star in the west.

He sat on the picnic table a little longer looking for more shooting stars, but there weren't any. It was getting even colder, and his nose was starting to drip.

Better get back in the truck and give Chris a call, he thought. *I can tell her I went to church tonight too.*

7

The Stockings Were Hung In the Rec Room

Cheryl picked up a pile of magazines from a basket in her living room and jammed them into a white plastic trash bag as Pentatonix belted out "Little Drummer Boy" on her radio.

She'd been listening to Christmas music for about an hour while she did some housekeeping, but after hearing "You're a Mean One, Mr. Grinch" four times in the same hour, she felt more cranky than ever.

She ran her fingers through her short black hair, stretched her lanky frame, and wondered what in the world was the matter with her.

Nothing was really wrong. She didn't know why she was so depressed this Christmas.

The fact that she didn't have a good answer made her even more edgy.

She usually enjoyed the holidays, but she certainly didn't have the

Christmas spirit this year. She'd just been going through the motions since Thanksgiving.

She'd battled the crowds at the mall, but her shopping was done. She'd worked until the wee hours of the morning for four days wrapping presents, but that was done too.

After a few trips to the 24-hour grocery store, late at night before the workers stocking the shelves had crushed their boxes, she had enough cartons for all the gifts she had to ship. She made four trips to the post office the Saturday two weeks before Christmas, but her shipping was done.

She always had problems printing out the mailing list for her Christmas cards because she didn't use Excel enough to feel comfortable with that software, but she'd accomplished that too. She'd inserted the cards and attached all the labels, stamped the envelopes, and put them into the mailbox at the post office in batches one night about 3 a.m.

She had hauled her Christmas decorations down from the attic right after Thanksgiving, and put the outdoor lights up one Sunday afternoon before the weather turned cold. They were on an automatic timer, and they'd been coming on every night since Dec. 10.

She hadn't gotten her artificial tree up the basement stairs yet, and the way she was feeling she might just skip that entirely this year. No company was coming, so she'd be the only person who would see it, and her house was so small that she could barely stand the clutter as it was.

She hadn't gotten around to baking any Christmas cookies, but her sister was the master baker anyway.

The Christmas mornings where Cheryl was bubbling over with enthusiasm for Santa's arrival were long gone, but she needed to get out of this funk.

She would go to mass on Christmas Eve and sleep in on Christmas morning. After her normal breakfast granola, she'd shower, pull on her best tailored gray pants and a sweater, add her grandmother's pearls, and steel herself for the duties ahead.

On Christmas afternoon she would drive to her parents' home about two hours away, put on a happy face, and deal with her know-it-all sister-in-law one more time.

She'd field at least one comment from her mother about why she wasn't dating anyone. She'd broken up with Steve two years ago, and she knew that was for the best. If she'd been committed to him for the rest of her life she'd be even more depressed.

But this wasn't helping.

Since Cheryl struggled with minor depression on and off, she knew that exercise, getting enough sleep, eating nutritious meals, and helping someone who was worse off than she was would help. And no matter how bad she felt, there was always someone who was worse off.

So, after a half-hour stint on her treadmill and a quick shower, she dialed her friend Mary Jean, who was a volunteer at a local center for the homeless.

"Sure, we'd be glad for your help!" Mary Jean said enthusiastically. "We're collecting socks to give out this month…the warmer the better!

"Quite a few businesses have been conducting sock drives for the holidays for about a month now," Mary Jean explained. "We need drivers to go pick up the socks from the businesses, and then deliver them to the two shelters in town."

"Give me a list, and I'll do it," Cheryl said willingly, if not enthusiastically.

After stops at three businesses on Mary Jean's list, the back of

Cheryl's blue hatchback was filled with cartons of socks. Most were brand-new, white athletic crew socks, but some hunting socks, some colorful knee socks, and some black, brown, and navy men's socks were in the mix too.

Since there was no more room in the car for any more boxes, Cheryl looked at the list for the name and address of the shelter she'd been assigned to deliver the socks. The East Side House of Hope was in a questionable area on the other side of the city, but after an hour of stop-and-go driving due to heavy traffic and construction, she was able to find a parking space in front of the shelter.

She stepped inside and tapped a small bell on a desk in the front hallway to summon the receptionist. Surely someone there could help her unload.

In about a minute an elderly black man with fuzzy gray hair appeared. He was wearing navy blue workpants and a black sweatshirt that asked, "Who's Pete Sake?"

"Can I help you?" he asked.

"I have socks donated by several businesses for you," she said. "Can you get someone to help me unload them?"

"You don't say," the man responded, looking doubtful. "What kind of socks?"

"All kinds of socks," Cheryl answered. "Weren't you expecting them?"

"Can't say as I knew anything about it," the man said with a shrug of his shoulders.

That was unfortunate, but Cheryl had a task to complete.

"Do you have a hand truck or a dolly that I could use?" she suggested.

"Can't say as I do," the old man said, looking a bit dismayed. "Mr.

Burt and Ms. Lillian aren't here right now," he informed her. "Only people here are me, some of the mothers, and a bunch of kids."

Mr. Burt and Ms. Lillian must be in charge, but Cheryl was not about to drive back across the city with a carload of socks.

Her informant had to be in his 80s. He shuffled more than he walked.

"Is there anyone else here who could help?" she suggested pleasantly.

"Can't say as there is," the man answered. "But maybe one of the mothers will help," he slowly added. "Let me go see."

He headed down a hallway, leaving Cheryl alone with her thoughts.

After a few minutes passed with no sign of him or any helpers, Cheryl propped the front door of the shelter open with a folding chair and went back to her car.

She had already brought two boxes in before the man and a woman who appeared to be in her late 20s appeared. The woman had skin the color of a copper skillet about a week after it's been polished. It contrasted greatly with her dyed, neon-pink hair.

She was wearing black sweatpants, an orange Notre Dame sweatshirt, and a lavender cap with studded rhinestones that spelled out "Sweetie Pie." She tottered on magenta pumps that easily had 4-inch heels.

Her silver hoop earrings were larger than the bangle bracelet surrounding Cheryl's left wrist. When the earrings flopped on opposite angles as she tilted her head to give Cheryl the once-over, Cheryl was reminded of an old TV with its antennas pushed off skew for the best reception.

"Doreen can help," the man said, nodding to the woman.

"What did you say you have in there? Socks?" Doreen was as clueless as the man.

"Yes, warm socks for the winter," Cheryl repeated, wondering why she was suddenly doubting the worth of the donation.

"You don't say," Doreen responded.

"Yes," Cheryl answered weakly.

"Well, I guess we can always use socks." Doreen seemed to be warming to the idea.

"Can you help me unload them?"

"Sure; no skin off my back," Doreen answered.

With both of them working, the job was completed in less than 10 minutes despite Doreen's enormously long, lime-green fingernails. Fourteen boxes of socks now stood in the shelter's entryway, and Cheryl's duty was done.

"Mama, what's in the boxes?" asked a boy who was peeking into the entryway, too shy to enter the room.

"Socks, she said," answered Doreen with a shrug towards Cheryl.

"You mean socks like we can hang up for Santa to fill?" asked the boy.

"Well, I guess we could do that," Doreen answered, "only don't get your hopes up because we should just be glad we got the socks."

Cheryl was almost out the door, but it was too late.

"How many children live here usually?" she asked the man.

"Oh, anywhere from 30 to 40," he answered, adding "Why?"

"I'll be back in about two hours," Cheryl said mysteriously. "Maybe Doreen can help me again then," she suggested.

Cheryl doubled-back to a dollar store and a grocery store near the interstate. She spent almost twice her total Christmas budget on stocking stuffers for some homeless kids that Christmas.

When she got back to the shelter a couple of hours later, Doreen helped her hide the bags of gifts in a hall closet. The elderly man locked it until they would open it on Christmas Eve.

As she was driving back to her house from the shelter, Cheryl found herself humming along to the radio station that played Christmas music 24/7.

After mass on Christmas Eve, Cheryl returned to the shelter around 11 p.m. The elderly man unlocked the closet, and Doreen led Cheryl to the shelter's large rec room.

Limp socks of every description hung from the mantle, bookcases, bulletin boards, and even the radiator. Cheryl laughed out loud when she saw an old pair of pantyhose thumb-tacked to the back of a chair. "Doreen" was scrawled on a piece of lilac notepaper taped to the chair above the pantyhose.

Cheryl, Doreen, and the elderly man got to work placing the gifts inside the socks. When they were finished the room almost glowed with lumpy socks hiding treasures like candy, oranges, note cards and even toothpaste.

As Cheryl drove to her parents' house on Christmas afternoon, she sang along to Christmas CDs on her car's audio system. Before she reached the halfway point she realized that somehow her Christmas spirit had returned.

She had definitely overspent this Christmas, but it was worth it for both her and for the residents of the East Side House of Hope.

8

Two Trees
For Two Brothers

Rick's cell phone dropped from his hand to the sofa that Thursday evening, and he hoped that what he'd just heard wasn't true.

But he knew it was.

His sister, Kathy, had the job of telling him. Their brother, Jeff, had been involved in a car accident that morning in Virginia, and he did not survive.

He did not survive.

Those four words repeated themselves over and over in Rick's brain as he tried to comprehend, but time was standing still.

Rick's 6-foot frame sank into the sofa cushions beside his phone. He didn't cry, swear or yell, but intense pain registered in his brown eyes. He was too numb to express his thoughts into words.

It was Dec. 18. He should be buying presents, stringing lights outside, attending Christmas concerts, and enjoying his Christmas tree, not dealing with grief and another funeral.

Another Christmas funeral.

He'd lost his eldest brother, Craig, due to a car accident in December of 2000. He hadn't fully recovered from that loss, which had tainted Christmas for him from that point on.

And now, 13 years later, they were going to do it all over again with Jeff.

What was God thinking? What does God have against my family? What does God have against me?

Trouble comes in threes. I'm the baby of three brothers. Now two of them are gone. Am I next?

How are my parents supposed to deal with this?

Rick shook his head. He wished he could yell. He wished he could cry. But all he could do was sit, staring blankly at a red-and-white wooden star on his Christmas tree.

He didn't bother with dinner. He fed the dogs, had a stiff drink, and then went to bed, hoping sleep would provide some escape.

But sleep would not come.

He called Kathy back in the morning. Since Jeff wasn't married, she was doing a lot of the work. She needed a few more telephone numbers to let some more family members know what had happened. He provided one she was missing, but she was always better than he was at keeping in touch with people anyway.

Rick asked about the accident. Jeff's pickup had tangled with a semi on his way to work. No alcohol or drugs were involved, and the weather was clear. No one else was hurt. The cops said he died instantly.

Mom and Dad were hanging in there. They all were. The funeral would be on the 27th, the Saturday after Christmas, to help everyone with small kids and those like him who had to travel.

"How are you doing, Rick?" Kathy wanted to know.

"I'll be OK; how are you?" Rick responded woodenly.

"One day at a time," was Kathy's wise answer.

Rick was an electrician. He called his boss at work, told him what had happened, and said he'd be out until Monday, if that was OK. He'd work Monday, Tuesday and Wednesday, which was Christmas Eve. He'd drive to Virginia on Christmas Day, and deal with the viewing on the 26th and the funeral on the 27th. He'd drive back home the day after the funeral, which was a Sunday, and be back at work again on the 29th.

His boss was an OK guy, and he was particularly nice about this. He told Rick that was fine, and expressed his condolences.

So now there was a schedule to this insanity.

Over the weekend, Rick tried to come to terms with what had happened. He spoke to Kathy at least daily. He was surprised but pleased when Tony, one of the guys from work, dropped off a casserole that his wife had made.

"It sucks, especially at Christmas," Tony said as he handed Rick the casserole through the gaping screen door. Rick accepted the casserole with one hand, as the other kept his dog Buster from running out the door, which was propped open by his foot.

"Come on in, man," Rick said.

Tony looked a little uncomfortable but Rick had to give him credit; he tried.

"We're all sorry," Tony started. "If there's anything we can do, just let us know."

"I'll be OK," Rick said as he put the casserole on his kitchen counter. "I'll be at work on Monday. I'll drive down there on Christmas Day. My next-door neighbors will feed the dogs and let them out while I'm gone."

So everything was set.

All he had to do was live through it.

Staying busy would help. The weather wasn't bad for December in Pennsylvania that weekend, so Rick climbed up on his ladder, took down his outdoor Christmas lights, and packed away the wreath and garland he'd hung on his front door.

He never sent Christmas cards, but he did have a few gift cards to give as presents to a few neighbors and friends. Since he didn't know when he'd see them, he bought a box of cards at the drug store, addressed them, popped the gift cards inside, stamped them and dropped them off in the outdoor mailbox in front of his local post office.

He also got a haircut and a trim of his short brown beard from a barber at the mall.

Another thing off his list.

Rick owned one suit. He never wore it, but he knew his mother would like to see him dressed properly for the occasion so he dragged it out of its garment bag in the spare bedroom and made sure it still fit. Luckily he could still button all the buttons, and with a white shirt and a dark tie he'd look as good as one of the undertakers.

As he worked, Rick's mind was spinning. Kathy had said Jeff died instantly. That was good. Craig had lingered in intensive care for two weeks before he died.

The three brothers had been close as children, and they were close as adults despite the intrusions of distance, jobs, and daily life. And now there was just he and Kathy. He needed to think less about his loss and more about his parents'.

When he was thinking straight, Rick knew that God hadn't caused Jeff's death. It wasn't like Noah's flood or anything. Just like God hadn't caused the diseases of the people who came to Jesus for healing, this was just something that had happened. He could either believe that or believe that God was out to get his family, and deep down he knew that wasn't the case. God was love, after all.

But he thought that even God would agree that the timing of this stunk.

Rick wasn't up to attending church that Sunday, but that afternoon he took down his Christmas tree and packed away all his decorations. Since he lived on a small farm, he'd taken a chainsaw to a Scotch pine at the back of the property for his tree this year. Now it lay near his burn barrel, and Christmas was still a week away.

That's probably the last Christmas tree I'll have, Rick thought. *It's the happiest time of the year for most everybody, but it just means grief to me.*

Rick had attended only four funerals in his life, and none had helped. He was glad some people found comfort in funerals, but all he wanted to do was to go trout fishing, and it was too cold for that.

He went through the motions at work on Monday, Tuesday, and Wednesday, glad for the distractions. All his co-workers knew about it via an e-mail from their boss. One at a time, all but two of them told him they were sorry, and asked if there was anything they could do. Rick figured the other two felt the same, but just didn't know how to express it.

On Christmas morning Rick threw his bag in the back of his SUV, hung the garment bag holding his suit on a hook in the back seat, hugged his dogs one more time, and headed south to say goodbye to his brother.

It wasn't fair. Christmas was for homecomings, not goodbyes.

The viewing was a blur. He remembered hugging relatives and friends, and choking down tuna casseroles at his parents' house. He slept in the twin bed in his old bedroom, and tried not to think about the empty bed beside it that had once been Jeff's.

He didn't know the new minister in town who would be conducting the funeral service. Their old minister, Pastor Rollins, had passed away more than five years ago of old age.

He was surprised to learn that the new minister was a young woman. That seemed far too progressive for such a small town in the heart of Virginia.

Rev. Janice Cunningham was her name. She seemed like a nice lady, and Rick tried to have an open mind.

Surprisingly she addressed some of his issues right away in her message.

"Christmas is supposed to be a time for fun, and not a time for death," she acknowledged. "When we lose someone close to us over the holidays, we feel cheated out of good times as well as cheated because we've lost someone close to us.

"But Christmas is more about a promise than it is about a good time, and that promise still holds, centuries later, because it's a promise from God," she continued. "That baby in the manger was a gift from God to save us so we will one day live again. Even as God was starting to put his promise into motion with the birth of that baby, He knew how His son would die, and yet He did it anyway. That love is something all of us can share in our relationship with Him.

"When you remember the grief you feel this Christmas, try also to remember the love that is at the heart of this holiday," she said. "Funerals seem the opposite of Christmas, but the Christmas story gives us the assurance that we'll see our loved ones again; that Christ loves us more than anything, and He is always there to help."

Rick thought about her words as he was driving back to Pennsylvania the following day. He still had a knot in his stomach, but he knew that would diminish with time.

Trying not to hate Christmas from now on was going to take some effort, though.

One Saturday morning the following fall, Rick got out his front-end loader and dug two holes at the entrance to his property, one on either side of his driveway. A local nursery delivered two blue spruces, and he helped the workers plant the trees in the holes he'd dug.

One was for Craig. The other was for Jeff.

They would be living memorials to remind him not only of his brothers, but also of God's great love at Christmas and the rest of the year too.

He decorated them each Christmas for the rest of his life.

9

Once Under a Mattress

Maria Victoria Ricardo Evangelista adjusted the uniform she wore as a member of the housekeeping staff and stood beside the king-size bed in Room 107 of the Hampton Inn and Suites, Indianapolis Airport.

She knew she could turn this mattress by herself, even if her name was longer than she was. She'd turned 50 on her last birthday, and she had come to terms with being 4-feet, 8-inches tall and just under 100 pounds a long time ago.

She pushed down on a corner of the pillow-top mattress with all her might. The opposite corner rose in the air, like the iceberg in front of the Titanic.

"If I give it one more big push, it will flip over," she thought confidently.

The mattress did flip over. It took Maria with it, pinning her between the mattress and the box spring.

"¡Socorro! Help!" she cried repeatedly, as the mattress was too heavy for her to move it off of her by herself.

Luckily she'd left the door to the room propped open by a doorstop, but no one was scheduled to check into this particular room for two days.

Someone will find me thought Maria, ever the optimist. *I will remain calm, and think of something else.*

And that's when Maria had an idea that solved a problem that had been nagging her for weeks.

Larry Fitzgerald was in his sweats, headed for a soda in the vending machine, when he heard a volley of Spanish as he ambled down the hotel's long hallway.

When he entered the room to investigate, Maria was still hollering, and her left arm and left leg were moving up and down like a marionette whose strings were being pulled by a drunk.

"Oh, gracias! Gracias!" Maria said when Larry pulled the mattress off her.

He truly was more surprised than she was.

It wasn't the first time Maria had gotten herself into a tight spot in the six months she'd worked in the hotel's housekeeping department.

Hotel guests would often do a double take when they saw her cart move by itself down the hallways. They eventually realized a tiny woman was pushing it and not a ghost.

The hotel manager had reprimanded her once for climbing into the hotel's huge dryer to retrieve a quarter, but that's the only way she could reach it.

Maria and her daughter-in-law, Sophia, both worked in housekeeping at the hotel. They'd relocated to Indianapolis from Dallas earlier in the year after Maria's son Juan, Sophia's husband, found work there with Federal Express. Indianapolis's mayor had conducted a campaign to attract Hispanic workers to fill many of the city's lower-paying jobs. It had proven to be a good opportunity.

The only problem was that most of the family was still in Dallas, and Maria had no idea how they'd all be able to be together for Christmas.

Maria's husband, Pedro, had passed away of cancer three years ago. Shortly thereafter Maria moved in with Sophia, Juan, and their two children, who had all made the move from Dallas to Indianapolis.

Two daughters — Camilla and Isabella— and one other son — Mateo — were still in Texas, and Maria's youngest son — Sebastian — was serving with the U.S. Army in Afghanistan.

All of them had children except for Sebastian. Money was tight, and the young mothers all wanted their children to be sleeping in their own beds when Santa came.

Even if her family could afford the transportation costs from Dallas to Indianapolis, Maria didn't know where they would all sleep. Sophia and Juan's new house in Indianapolis was only a three-bedroom house; their two children were already sharing one bedroom.

But while she was under that mattress, Maria realized she already knew of a place with more than three beds. After all, she was under the mattress of one of them.

The answer had literally hit her in the face.

That afternoon she talked her plan over with her manager and learned that the hotel offered a special employee rate that would make the family's stay affordable.

She got permission to use the conference room for their meals, and there would already be a big Christmas tree in the lobby! The kids could go swimming in the hotel's indoor pool, too!

Maria called her family that night, suggesting that everyone meet in Indianapolis on Dec. 27. She sent an e-mail to Sebastian overseas to invite him too. A day later he responded that he'd be unable to get leave this year, but all the Dallas-based family would come!

Maria and some of the other ladies who worked at the hotel decorated the big Christmas tree in the lobby, positioning it near the
property's gigantic gas fireplace. Maria purchased red silk poinsettias
from a discount store to add to the mix, and she placed the family's
treasured nativity scene under the tree for all to enjoy.

Maria gladly worked a 10-hour shift on Christmas Day, and she
switched with a co-worker and worked an eight-hour stint the day
after Christmas too.

Her family started to arrive that evening. Bobby James, who drove
the hotel shuttle, picked up the ones that were flying. Maria picked
the others up at the bus station early the next morning in Sophia's
van, sitting on a plastic wedge in order to reach the pedals and still
peer out the windshield.

Maria had a special Christmas piñata for the children to enjoy
before Christmas dinner was served. The dinner itself may have been
two days late, and served out of crockpots in the hotel's conference
room, but it was delicious. The smell of tamales, atole, buñuelos, and
ham permeated the first floor of the hotel. Sophia even made her special ponche, a traditional Mexican fruit drink.

All of the children had packed their swimsuits, and they enjoyed
the indoor pool that afternoon. There was a little argument when
two of the boys tried to stage luggage-cart races, and Isabella made
her daughters have a "time out" after a pillow fight, but the gathering
had almost all the components of home.

Sebastian spoke to them all one by one via Skype in the hotel's
business center during a conversation that took over an hour. The
connection dropped once, but one of Maria's 12-year-old, tech-savvy
grandkids got him back.

Maria's children pooled their resources to get her a gift certificate to a nearby spa for Christmas, but her greatest gift truly was her family being together for the holidays.

"Thank you for making Christmas so special," Sophia whispered to her as they watched the children play in the lobby.

Maria looked at her grandchildren playing, and her children enjoying their visit. She gave a sigh of satisfaction, knowing that her inspiration while caught under a mattress had generated a wonderful holiday for her family, and she loved each of them tremendously.

"I just went for the mattresses; I do my best work in bed," she said to Sophia with a smile.

10

Over the River and Through the Woods

Michelle slid open the big white barn door, a red lead line hidden behind her back, and looked around the pasture.

Luckily the horses were still nearby, munching on flakes of hay that the barn's manager, Penny, had distributed around the water tub. It wouldn't be hard for Michelle to catch Johnny, her husband's coal-black Tennessee Walker.

Johnny dutifully followed her back into the barn. Her own Thoroughbred-Quarter horse cross, Stallone, looked at her quizzically for a few seconds and then bent down to resume nibbling on his flake of hay.

The two horses were completely different in temperament. Stallone was definitely a type "A" personality, as he was more than a little high strung. Johnny was a type "B." He'd been used as a trail horse all his life, and he was definitely the safer choice for today's assignment.

Today was the day of Running Ridge Farm's Christmas party, and Michelle planned to arrive on horseback instead of in a car. Her husband had to work that Saturday, but she felt confident she'd have no problems taking Johnny on the short hack through the woods, down the towpath of the old canal, and into the main gate of the Thoroughbred farm now leased by her friend Jenny. Although Michelle hadn't told Jenny of her plans, she knew there were plenty of vacant stalls in Jenny's barn where Johnny could stay while she was at the party.

So, with Christmas carols on the barn's boom box for accompaniment and two barn cats for company, Michelle groomed Johnny thoroughly and then tacked him up.

She had locked her purse in the trunk of her car in the parking lot of the small, private stable. Her ID, her car key, a little bit of cash, her cell phone, a brush and a hoof pick were securely hidden in various pockets of the photographer's vest underneath her jacket. After turning off the radio and saying a quick goodbye to the cats, she led Johnny out front, slid the barn's front door closed, and used a mounting block to climb aboard.

Johnny danced around just a little as he left the comfort of the barn without his buddies. That was good, because it gave her the opportunity to slide off him and retighten his girth. Johnny was no dummy, and he blew up his belly every time he was tacked up. With the girth tightened a little more now, she remounted and was off.

Michelle thought she might be in trouble when Stallone and two other horses galloped to the fence to see them off, but Johnny remained pointed in the right direction and seemed to have accepted his assignment.

Although New Jersey was often cloudy and gray in the winter, this morning was one of those brilliant winter days when the sun was shining and the sky was bluer than blue. The air was crisp, and both Michelle and Johnny made water vapor when they exhaled. It had snowed about an inch overnight, blanketing the ground with fresh, clean snow. The snow had the consistency of Michelle's mom's homemade icing when she put a little too much sugar in the bowl. Michelle liked that little bit of crunch in both her icing and her snow.

Johnny walked along nicely as they passed the end of the pasture and headed for the woods. They'd both done this part of the trip many times. It was a short ride to a clearing cut into the woods for a big electrical tower of some sort. They'd be able to take that path for about 20 minutes before they had to veer off into solid woods.

Michelle peered over Johnny's ears, which swiveled to attention now and then as he explored sounds she could hear and many she couldn't. Since she knew the ground was smooth in this section, she trotted for a little bit just to get their blood up. Johnny responded eagerly, and both felt glad to be alive on such a beautiful morning.

Michelle dropped him back to a walk at the electrical tower, and they started the slight decline down a hill, towards the woods. Although there were no leaves on the trees there were a few evergreens, and it was definitely darker than the cleared trail. Michelle knew there were some stones here and there too, buried in the snow, so she gave Johnny some rein. He was sure-footed and not prone to stumbling, but she was taking no chances.

Suddenly Johnny erupted into a series of bounces, as did four deer that had been bedded down in some mountain laurel next to the trail. Michelle didn't have time to know for certain, but she thought at least one of the deer was a buck as four tan bodies exploded around her, their ears and white tails at attention. She grabbed Johnny's mane and the reins got a bit tangled, but she never lost her stirrups, and Johnny stopped after only about eight bounces.

As Michelle regrouped, she was glad she was on Johnny. She knew she'd have been on the ground now, watching Stallone gallop off without her, if she'd ridden him.

She patted Johnny's neck as he looked in the direction where the deer had disappeared.

"My, that was exciting!" she told him. "Thanks for not dumping me!"

They proceeded through the woods with no other excitement, crossed a two-lane road that was deserted at the moment, and headed towards the towpath of the old D&R Canal at Griggstown.

The canal was built in the 1830s to transport supplies between New York and Pennsylvania. Today it was primarily used for water supply and recreation.

The local horse and pony club had carved several loops free of brush off the canal and the adjoining Millstone River for trail riding, and they kept most of those trails cut back of vegetation. Michelle was sticking to the towpath today, however, because the farm she was visiting was just ahead.

Within minutes she crossed a bridge, traveled along the road for a few strides, and entered her friend's property. The whole ride had taken a little more than an hour.

Eight cars were parked in the driveway as Michelle and Johnny headed to the barn. She dismounted and had already led Johnny inside when her friend Jenny entered the barn to greet her.

"I can't believe you rode here! That's so cool!" Jenny said.

"It was fun; we came across some deer but we didn't have any problems," Michelle said with a smile.

After unsaddling, Michelle gave Johnny a quick brush and she picked out all four of his hooves with her hoof pick. Jenny told her which stall to put him in, and she made sure there was a pail of fresh water and two flakes of hay inside. As long as there was hay, Johnny was happy.

With that, the two friends went inside the house. Michelle made a quick trip to the powder room to rinse a bit of mud off, and then greeted the group assembled for the party. She knew most of them from horse activities anyway, and they were all pleased with her choice of transportation.

"It was fun, but I'm glad I have a car too," Michelle said. "I can't imagine what it would have been like to ride a horse or take a carriage everywhere, like in the old days. It would take so long to do anything!"

"Hey, what about having to ride a donkey all the way from Nazareth to Bethlehem when you're pregnant?" added her friend Nena. "I read that's like 70 or 90 miles!"

A wide variety of hors d'oeuvre, Christmas cookies, and beverages were offered, and the conversation was light as the party-goers visited and remarked about the beautifully-decorated house.

Michelle stayed a little over an hour because she didn't want to be on the trails at night. Although she was personable, she wasn't particularly skilled at small talk, so an hour was perfect. At most parties Michelle usually played with the family dog to avoid conversations, but she'd been more social than usual today.

After she said her goodbyes and returned to the barn, she found Johnny finishing the last traces of his hay. It was a shame to disturb him, but duty called.

Jenny followed her out to the barn. She watched her friend tack up, and bid her goodbye from the barn door.

As Michelle and Johnny retraced their steps, they encountered more activity on the towpath this time. They came across a couple that was cross-country skiing, as well as two hardy joggers. Soon the towpath was behind them though, and they headed back into the woods.

Although it was still afternoon, the woods were decidedly darker than they'd been in the morning. They kicked a couple of pheasants out of some brush, but they were far enough ahead that Johnny just stopped to look at them and then proceeded. They didn't see any more deer, but they saw a couple of rabbits, and Michelle thought she saw a small fox slink away near the electrical tower.

Every horse at the barn greeted them at the fence as they got home, probably because it was about time for the second feeding of the day. Johnny remained on his best behavior throughout, and Michelle gave him a thorough grooming before she turned him into his stall with his evening grain, a fresh bucket of water, hay, and several carrots. She then opened the barn door to the pasture, and the rest of the horses dutifully filed into their respective stalls for the suppers awaiting them.

She closed all the stall doors, made quick calls to both Jenny and her husband to ensure them that she'd arrived safely, finished a few last-minute chores, and prepared to call it a day.

The sun was just beginning to set in a gorgeous array of colors as Michelle left the barn, tired but with a Christmas memory that she'd never forget.

11

The Tree House
And the Butterfly

Brent Thompson sank into the cushy brown leather of the recliner in his contemporary, light blue-and-white, beachfront bedroom and pressed the small silver button on the right side.

His athletic body slowly reclined. His feet, encased in tan slippers, simultaneously rose on the footrest. He settled even deeper into the cushions as he gazed out the bedroom's French doors. A few steps beyond a deck would take him to a generous pool and adjoining hot tub. A white-sand beach and a gentle surf beckoned a short walk beyond the pool.

He sighed contentedly as he lowered headphones down over his ears. After a quick glance at his $14,000 watch, he absentmindedly took a sip of a vodka tonic, and then placed the monogrammed, double old-fashioned glass back on the end table to the right of the recliner. He smoothed his thick brown hair with his right hand, lowered his eyes, and used his left hand to click the remote on the expensive stereo system that took up most of the chrome bookcase to his left.

Within seconds, violins captured at a concert halfway around the world some 21 years ago joined the sound of the waves gently touching the shoreline and the occasional seagull's calls in the distance.

Always an aficionado of culture, Brent loved classical music. He'd become enamored with "The Butterfly Lovers Violin Concerto" by Yu Lina on a recent trip to Acheng, China. The preliminary drawings for a 10-story railway station his company was building in Acheng had been approved right before Christmas. With the stress of his workload and the cultural differences that he'd faced at every turn, he was glad to be spending a quiet Christmas at the four-bedroom home he'd designed himself in Melbourne, Florida. Some of his staff members were spending the holidays skiing in Switzerland and Canada, but he was more than content to be having a tropical Christmas at home in Florida with his wife, Liz; 8-year-old son, Matt, and 6-year-old daughter, Jessica.

Brent had been the lead architect for Mansfield, Bruce, Slease, and Stewart for more than 10 years, and he was proud of the buildings he designed. His latest project would be constructed primarily of glass and steel, and it would continue the Western feeling being established in the revitalized section of the city. The building would feature the latest environmental technology available and a unique lobby with huge glass elevators and several waterfalls. He planned to submit his drawings for several awards when construction was complete a year from now. He had a good feeling about the building's prospects. Other buildings he'd designed in the past had been award winners, and he thought this newest project was his best work ever.

It had been a whirlwind to get everything approved before Christmas, but now he had nearly a month at home before an intensive slate of meetings would start in preparation for the company's next big project.

As the concerto continued to the Pastoral track, Brent relaxed totally. His eyelids closed over his deep brown eyes and he was in the zone right before sleep when suddenly he felt, more than heard, someone in the room.

His son, Matt, was in the doorway, cautiously looking in. Normally Matt's head was down, as he played video games constantly, but right now it was up, and Brent could plainly see that his son wanted to ask him something.

Matt cleared his throat and then timidly said, "Dad?"

"Yes?" Brent asked as he shifted in the recliner to see his son more clearly.

"I was just wondering…." Matt began, and then his voice drifted off.

"I was just wondering," he repeated, "if maybe we could build a tree house out back while you're home for Christmas."

"A tree house?" Brent questioned.

"I just thought it would be cool to have one," Matt said, apologetically.

"I think that would be fun," Brent lied. He'd planned to spend a great deal of his time off on the golf course and in his catamaran. Building a tree house hadn't been on his itinerary.

But it was Christmas, the perfect time for family activities, and Brent knew his long absences weren't easy for any of them.

So the next Saturday morning, right after breakfast, Brent and Matt got busy. Brent took a yellow legal pad out of his briefcase, placed it on the granite countertop of the island in the kitchen, and used his favorite sterling silver pen to take notes. He treated Matt like his best client, and posed his typical leading questions about design, form, and function for the tree house project.

"I think it would be great to have a place to get away from Jessica," Matt said in answer to the "function" question. "She's always following me around, and she hears everything."

"I do not!" yelled Jessica from the living room, making both Brent and Matt smile.

From there they headed to the back yard to take a look at the job site.

Brent had been raised on a farm in rural Wisconsin that had a large, wooded back yard. He'd spent many happy hours reading while sprawled in the branches of a large oak tree during his youth.

Matt wasn't so lucky. A scrubby sand pine tree in the corner of the property, a little beyond the hot tub, looked like the only option to host Matt's tree house.

But Brent was determined to make it special. After several more meetings that they kept top secret from Liz and Jessica, Brent prepared an actual blueprint of the construction plans, they made a list of materials, and headed to a home-improvement store for supplies.

Brent had forgotten how much he enjoyed working with his hands. It had been years since he'd used a saw, and he relished the tactile feel and smell of freshly cut lumber. He'd loved carpentry as a teenager and as a young man. It had fueled his interest in architecture, but he'd gotten away from the basics of the craft as his career progressed.

He found that he liked sharing his love of carpentry with Matt. He liked showing him the right way to hold tools, and he stressed the importance of measuring twice before cutting to avoid mistakes. Due to Brent's work schedule the pair had never before shared such a big project, and Brent knew they were making memories in addition to a tree house.

The tree house itself was a masterpiece. Since the sand pine tree was so skimpy and the soil so sandy, they built the tree house on stilts firmly entrenched in cement.

They continued to keep their plans a secret from Liz and Jessica, which created a further bond between the builders. As the features took shape, the pride they had for their handiwork increased.

Access to the tree house wasn't via a ladder, but a full staircase complete with a turn and a landing. They found some windows on Craigslist at a low price, so the tree house had an actual double-pane window on each side instead of simply a hole. A special-order Dutch door that someone had returned to the home-improvement store provided the primary access. A second-hand sliding door at the back opened onto a small deck that faced the ocean, complete with a railing. It was all made from pressure-treated lumber.

The little sand pine tree was dwarfed by it all, and each day Brent and Matt grew a little closer as they worked together.

Brent was surprised when Matt posed a question about religion one afternoon as they were staining the staircase. It came totally out of the blue.

"Dad, do you think Jesus worked with Joseph too? Joseph was a carpenter, you know," Matt asked.

"I'm sure he did," Brent replied.

"Then why didn't he just become a carpenter when he grew up, instead of being a preacher that ended up getting killed?" Matt asked.

Brent had been raised a Lutheran. Although he felt he was a Christian, the truth was his faith had taken a back seat all his adult life. It wasn't that he didn't believe. He was glad to have been raised as a churchgoer, but religion just didn't seen relevant to his current adult life.

But he thought he came up with a pretty good answer, considering.

"Well, Jesus was God's son as well as Joseph's son," Brent pointed out. "He had a bigger job to do than to build things."

"He had to show everybody how to live, and then he died to save people from going to hell, right?" Matt asked.

"There's more to it than that, but that about sums it up," Brent concurred. "His basic message was to believe in God, love one another, try to live a good life, and forgive people when they do you wrong."

Matt was silent as he continued to work his paintbrush over the staircase, deep in thought.

"I'm glad we're building this tree house," Matt said. "I need to have a place to get away from Jessica. She's been going on and on about her dumb lost reindeer. She thinks I took it, but I didn't. I don't know why she carries a reindeer around all the time anyway, even in the summer."

"Hopefully Ginger will turn up," Brent said, hoping his son was telling the truth about the stuffed toy. "And I'm glad we're building the tree house too," he added, and he meant it. The time he had spent with his son was much more important than classical music, golf with the neighbors, or even time on the water with his catamaran.

When the tree house was finished a few days later, they had a party to celebrate. Jessica had developed a case of strep throat, so they humored her and had a tea party in her bedroom. They sat on tiny pink chairs surrounding a tiny white circular table, and ate Christmas cupcakes with red frosting and green sprinkles. Jessica's toy reindeer had turned up that morning, so peace was restored at the Thompsons' house in time for Christmas.

Matt and two of his friends spent the first of many nights in the tree house that night. Even the tree house was decorated for Christmas, with plastic garland on the staircase and a big pine wreath on the top half of the Dutch door.

Later that night, before Liz came up to bed, Brent relaxed in his recliner and pushed the button on his stereo system's remote once again. The strains of "The Butterfly Lovers Violin Concerto" filled the night air. As if it had been waiting in the wings for a cue, a yellow butterfly appeared suddenly outside the window and rested on the deck's railing for a few measures before it fluttered away.

Brent settled back in his recliner with a contented smile. He was happier than he'd ever been. No matter where he traveled throughout the world, he was grateful that he had a home and family to return to for the holidays. He'd always consider the year of the tree house and the butterfly to be his best Christmas ever.

12

Ginger, Come Home!

With a loud thump and the sickening sound of shattering glass, Liz Thompson backed her black Porsche Cayenne into the side of a silver BMW in the mall parking lot.

"Are you OK, Jess?" she demanded of her 6-year-old daughter strapped into a child car seat in the back.

"We're OK, Mommy," said Jessica, clutching her favorite toy, a stuffed reindeer named Ginger.

Liz had been trying to leave the mall parking lot after picking up a new video game for her 8-year-old son, Matt, for Christmas.

She never saw the BMW before she hit it, but she'd never forget the volley of swear words its driver released on her for wrecking into his brand-new car.

"It's not like I did it on purpose," she said as she tried to calm him down. "The important thing is no one was hurt. We'll exchange insurance info and everything will be OK."

She said the same thing to the driver of the mall security car who appeared almost immediately after the accident, and again to the local police officer who responded to his call.

She hadn't been going fast as she backed out of her parking space, but the back of her car had done a lot of damage to the left side of the BMW. The damage included one of its expensive, custom black wheels that she learned had been installed that morning after almost a three-month delay in customs. The now-damaged BMW was supposed to be a Christmas gift for the driver's wife.

She had hit him square. Both of the taillights on her car were destroyed, the tailgate was both scraped and dented, and her bumper now hung at an angle.

"I'm truly very sorry," she said for the countless time, fighting back tears.

Just when it looked like things couldn't get any worse, they did.

"Where is my wallet?" she gasped after the police officer asked to see her license, registration, and insurance card. The registration and insurance card were in the glove box, but her wallet — holding her license, the bulk of her Christmas money, and all her credit cards — was definitely not in her purse.

"I've been robbed!" she sobbed.

The BMW required a tow truck but her own car could still be driven, so Liz and Jessica followed the police officer to his barracks to file a report about the missing wallet. They all knew it was useless but they went through the procedure anyway, and then Liz and Jessica carefully returned to their seaside home in Melbourne, Florida.

Unfortunately Liz's unlucky streak continued in the week ahead.

The paperwork to replace her driver's license and credit cards was tedious and annoying.

Somehow she missed an appointment for a house showing for the first time in her career as a real-estate agent, forcing her to apologize profusely, and her boss gave her a strange look.

A closing she'd counted on to put her over her annual sales goals was postponed until January due to a stubborn seller, so she wouldn't be getting her bonus.

Then she was embarrassed to learn that the Christmas cards she'd mailed the day before the accident didn't have enough postage on them.

After watching for her letter carrier for over an hour, she let him have it.

"Who knew that square envelopes cost more to mail than rectangular ones?" she demanded. She was mortified that everyone on her list was getting notices in their mailboxes of postage due. In order to receive her family's Christmas greeting, they'd have to trek to their local post office during regular business hours, and sign for her Christmas card after paying an additional 7 cents.

Her in-laws telephoned to announce that they'd be coming to visit the day after Christmas, and would stay at least a week. At least her husband, an architect who did a great deal of work overseas, would be home by then.

Liz was used to an absentee husband; it had been that way almost since day one of their marriage. But his long absences were a strain on the entire family. It seemed they'd just get used to him being home when he'd leave again.

Liz didn't want to complain, but she often felt she was mother and father to everyone, including her husband. The last time Brent was home he spent far too much time with his golfing buddies for her tastes, and if he did it again at Christmas she could feel a fight brewing.

Brent had a good-paying job, and the family didn't have to worry about money, but that didn't mean she should have to handle everything else on her own in this partnership.

With her car in the shop, Liz rented a SUV to continue her daily shuttle service to her kids' numerous lessons and practices. Although Matt spent most of his life playing video games, he was also learning to play the trumpet, and he was on a local soccer team. Jessica begged daily for horseback riding lessons, but so far Liz and Brent had just agreed to piano lessons and tap class for the baby of the family.

Two nights before her husband was due to arrive, Liz was struggling to find gift boxes while wrapping presents on the granite island in her gourmet kitchen. She felt like she might be coming down with a cold. She already had a pounding headache after Matt's half-hour practice session with his trumpet, which consisted of loud scales, something that sounded like a march, and plenty of mistakes.

At dinner Matt had casually mentioned that he needed 24 Christmas cupcakes for a party at school tomorrow afternoon. She'd either have to whip them up tonight or get everyone up earlier tomorrow so they could stop at the bakery before school. Jessica was pouting because she couldn't find her stuffed reindeer, Ginger. Matt had gone back to his video games after his time at the trumpet, but now he was teasing Jessica unmercifully for being a baby about the toy. Jessica was in tears, and Liz was ready to explode.

"Matt, be nice!" she snapped. "Jessica, where is the last place you saw Ginger?"

"I don't know, Mommy!" Jessica wailed. "I think maybe he was on the stairs."

"We'll all look for him, and that includes you, Matt," Liz announced.

Ginger was about 10 inches tall and about 7 inches wide. Despite the fact that Jessica had given him a feminine name, they all referred to Ginger as a "he" because he had antlers. He was tan with brown features, and he had green inner ears. He wore a bright red, silk bow. His eyes were tiny and deep set above his snout, and he sported a perpetual grin in brown embroidery. He'd been part of a Christmas floral arrangement sent to her husband by a business associate last year, and Jessica loved him instantly.

Unfortunately Ginger remained lost the rest of that night, and Jessica cried herself to sleep without him. The next day they turned the house upside down looking for him, but he was still missing the following afternoon when they all piled in the rental car to head to the airport to pick up Brent.

The reunion was a happy one, but Brent seemed especially tired after the long series of flights from his latest assignment in China. He retired to their bedroom early, and he was asleep by the time Liz joined him, but before she headed for bed she had heard the strains of violins coming from the sound system in their room.

The next morning Brent and Matt were huddled together, discussing something, but Liz chocked that up to Christmas secrets. She still had a great deal to do to get ready for Christmas, and Jessica was still fretting over the missing Ginger.

"Honey, I'm sure he's here somewhere," Liz told her. "He'll turn up sometime!"

But Ginger remained M.I.A.

On Saturday morning Brent and Matt continued to conspire about something, and it eventually came out that they were planning to build a tree house in the back yard.

Liz was glad to see Brent taking an interest in Matt.

Jessica, however, was not amused.

"Matt gets to do everything!" she complained, as her lower lip trembled. "It's just because he's 8. I never get to do anything fun!"

"Well, complaining right before Christmas won't help matters," Liz pointed out.

Jessica stomped up to her room and slammed the door.

"Nice," Liz said to no one in particular.

Jessica continued to be on her worst behavior as the tree house took shape and Christmas approached. One afternoon when Liz was trying to decide what to make for dinner, she found that Jessica had gotten into her makeup and painted eyebrows and cheeks on the family cat, Mittens. Poor Mittens even had a streak of red lipstick around her mouth before Liz rescued her.

"Jessica, what's wrong with you? You know you shouldn't have done that to Mittens!" Liz scolded.

"I don't know, Mommy," Jessica muttered. "I just feel like being bad."

"Well you better snap out of it right away," Liz advised her. "Santa is watching!"

Jessica came down with a sore throat the following day, which was pronounced as strep throat by her pediatrician the next afternoon.

Brent and Matt finished the tree house a couple days later, but not after tracking sand and sawdust over the living room carpet. But Liz had to admit the tree house was the best-looking one she'd ever seen.

By that time the antibiotics Jessica was taking had begun to work, so they celebrated the end of the tree house's construction and tried to cheer Jessica up with a tea party in Jessica's bedroom.

The family of four, including Brent, sat on tiny pink chairs in Jessica's room, and Jessica served them lemonade out of a teapot decorated with pink tulips. The main course was devil's food cupcakes complete with red frosting and green sprinkles. The chocolate combined with the lemonade provided a definite punch to the palate.

And in the place of honor, seated in his own chair at the tiny table, too short to be anywhere close to eye level, was the long-missing Ginger.

"Where did you find him?" Liz wanted to know.

"He fell down behind the bookcase; he was in my room the whole time," Jessica informed them, happily licking red frosting off the top of her cupcake.

"Well, I'm certainly glad he's home!" Liz exclaimed. "I'm glad we're all home, and happy, at Christmas, despite how stressful the holidays can be," she said.

Deep in her heart Liz knew that although her family rarely if ever acknowledged it, she was the glue that held them together. Although it was hard to see past the often-frustrating challenges of her daily life, everything had changed when she became a mother.

"I love you all more than anything," she said as she looked at the happy smiles around the tiny table, and she meant every word.

13

'Merry Christmas, Emily'

Bobby Gaines considered eating one of the sugar cookies on the plate his nephews had prepared for Santa, but thought better of it.

What he really wanted was a drag from one of his cigarettes, but he never smoked in his brother's house and the sub-freezing temperatures of a Boston winter night made it much too cold to sit outside.

The brownstone was quiet. Bobby's back ached, but he tried to ignore the pain.

Bobby's brother and sister-in-law had already assembled the toys that needed assembling, put their gifts under the Christmas tree in preparation for the morning, and were in bed.

Their boys were also in bed, but they hadn't gone without a struggle. Last Christmas morning they ran down the stairs at 4 a.m., thrilled to see that Santa had paid his annual visit on schedule.

The overhead lights were off but the tree's lights were still on, casting a beautiful glow over the room. Bobby sat on the buttery leather sofa for a few minutes, just drinking the scene in. The candles were out, but the rich aroma of scented wax still hung in the air.

It was such a perfect scene, so unlike his life. Things had been out of control for a long time, and he was too numb to do anything about it.

Everything had been so promising before the accident.

He had been racing 410 sprint cars on a national level, and he was beginning to get noticed. He was a hit with the fans, and especially the ladies.

The day before the accident, Old Man Saunders had finally called him. He told him to come over to his car dealership the following Wednesday to talk about running his sprint car on the World of Outlaws circuit next season.

Saunders had great equipment, a top crew chief, good engines, and deep pockets. It was the opportunity of a lifetime, but it was an appointment Bobby was never able to keep.

He didn't remember the wreck, but he had seen it a few times on YouTube.

Ironically it happened at his favorite track, Williams Grove Speedway in Mechanicsburg, Pennsylvania.

He had been on the outside, trying to pass a lapped car, when he hooked wheels with the slower driver and went into a series of hard, vicious flips. After he cleared the outside guardrail between Turns 1 and 2 he continued to flip. What was left of his car finally came to rest near some outbuildings outside the track, upside down.

Luckily there was no fire, but Bobby had been knocked out cold.

The list of injuries was so long, it was lucky he lived. He knew that. But the pain was so bad most days that he wished he hadn't.

After the volunteer rescue crew reached him, they called for a helicopter to take him to the regional trauma center.

He remained in intensive care there for four months, and he hadn't raced since. Each day — and year — that passed made a return to the cockpit less likely.

He'd undergone 11 operations. His left leg was permanently shorter than the right one now so he walked with a limp, but at least he could still walk.

The list of his injuries had been impressive. He had a couple of spinal fractures, a punctured lung, all of his ribs were broken, and there was bleeding around his heart. There was a head injury to deal with. Both of his legs and both of his arms were broken, and he almost died one more time when he got pneumonia about a month later.

God had let him live, so there must be some plan.

But rehab was hell on earth.

Somehow he'd come out the other side, but not before becoming addicted to his pain medication. And that's when the trouble really started. He'd been in jail a couple of times, primarily for possession.

It wasn't that he wanted to get high just for the hell of it. He needed to be high to handle the pain.

Most of his friends had slowly disappeared. He didn't blame them; they had lives to live. It wasn't their fault that he couldn't live the life he wanted anymore.

He tried not to think about his once-promising future. He had loved the travel and camaraderie of track life. Throughout his career he drove hard and he played harder, and he knew it was just a matter of time until he'd become a star. He'd practiced signing his signature for hours until he got it perfect for autographs. He'd worked on his victory-lane speeches in the shower.

Now all he had was pain and regrets.

One of his crew members who visited him in the hospital told him at least he could say he lived life with no regrets.

But that friend was wrong. Bobby had plenty of regrets. He figured if a person didn't have regrets, he should have gotten out more.

Bobby was down to just a few friends now. One of them, a girl named Emily who worked in timing and scoring at Williams Grove, texted him every day when he was in the hospital just to let him know he hadn't been forgotten, but he usually ignored her messages. Now and then he'd reply, but mostly he just drifted in and out of touch.

Emily was not the type of girl that interested him, but she was nice. She was a little plump, she wore glasses, and she had short, light-brown hair done up in tight curls all over her head. She worked full-time as a dental hygienist.

She always sent him a Christmas card in care of his mother, and included a little gift.

He knew his lack of communication annoyed her.

At first she left a polite message on his cell phone saying that not hearing from him made her feel taken advantage of.

Once she told him off forcefully via a notecard, ending with an ultimatum that he should think about other people more than himself.

Last Christmas she sent him a check for $25 and instructions to buy a phone card at the drug store and give her a call.

He waited a couple of months and then cashed her check, but he never called.

He did always text her on her birthday, usually at 2:30 a.m. when he knew she'd be asleep. It wasn't hard to remember the date, since it was in August, around the same time as his accident.

After the check-cashing incident he wouldn't have blamed her if she had written him off for good, but a couple of weeks ago a small package arrived for him at his mom's house, just like in years past. It contained a small journal and a Christmas card.

"This not communicating stinks," she wrote on the card. "How are you?"

Part of him wanted to talk to her, but he was afraid it would only make him feel worse. She was a nice girl, and she didn't deserve any of his bullshit. So he didn't call, although he wished he had every day.

And now it was Christmas Eve.

He flipped on the TV to listen to Christmas mass from the Vatican. Bobby had been raised a Catholic, and despite all his problems he still believed.

This latest pope sure was an optimist. He spoke of God's unending love, and the power of forgiveness.

And he emphasized that Christmas was a good time to let people know how much they meant to you.

He said it was also a great time for new beginnings.

Before he could talk himself out of it, Bobby dialed the cell phone number he knew by heart.

She wouldn't recognize his number when it came up on the display since he was using his brother's phone. It was late, so if she didn't answer at least he'd leave a voicemail.

"Hello?" Her voice was clear but questioning.

"Merry Christmas, Emily," he began.

About the Author

Apparently the holidays have always amazed Linda. Here she is with her mother on her very first Christmas.

Linda Mansfield and some of her girlfriends are rewriting the stereotype of single women who live with cats.

Linda and her two cats live in Indianapolis, the world center of motorsports. She has a decidedly non-traditional job as the public relations representative of several top auto racing teams and drivers through her company, Restart Communications. Her family also includes a retired Morgan horse who lives in Missouri, but that's another story.

Linda is originally from Pennsylvania, where her sister, Karen, still lives. Karen is the family's expert baker of Christmas cookies, continuing a tradition made famous by their mother.

Linda has many years of experience as a reporter, writer, and editor, including time on the copy desk of a Manhattan publishing house. Although she's edited six books for other authors, this is the first one she's written herself. For information on what she's working on next, see LindaMansfieldBooks.com. For information about her racers, see RestartCommunications.com. Her Facebook page is at "Linda Mansfield — Author," and she's @RestartLMAuthor on Twitter.

If you enjoyed this book, please write a good review!

Linda, her family and friends wish you and yours a very Merry Christmas!

Don't miss the other books in the "Two Good Feet" series!

1

2

3

4

CPSIA information can be obtained
at www.ICGtesting.com
Printed in the USA
LVHW102333101022
730421LV00004B/221

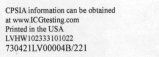

9 780996 243315